THE FRAGRANCE OF DANCE

By

Minister Tramona Ford

First Printing, 2015

ISBN 978-0-692-45008-6

Book Production: Maple Press Printing Company, York PA

Cover design by Kevin Vain- KDV Design & Associates @ www.kdvdesign.com

Contact Author @ tfordwpraize91@gmail.com

Workshops

Ministry in Dance

Preaching

"We feel privileged to endorse Rev.Tramona's book. You will find it to be a source of information, and instruction, but even more it will stir your heart to worship and to live a life of holiness; a life that would become a sweet aroma unto the Lord."
Drs. Wendell and Juanita Burden-Pastors of Family Life Ministries Int.

"The Fragrance of Dance has a deeply inspirational and scriptural approach to the meaning of worshipping God through dance. The author covers topics and aspects of priesthood and prophetic dance on a new and revelational level that every person called to this art form should absorb. Thereby, the knowledge acquired from reading this study, about when we offer up our sacrifice of praise through movement, will take the reader to new depths of transformational understanding."
Pastor Lynn M. Hayden-Dancing for Him Ministries

" Tramona Ford has captured the essence of worship as a fragrance via dance from a unique perspective as she overlays the role of the Levites from a Jewish prospective to the worshippers who present offerings in the 21st century.... their mandate should release a pure fragrance of worship."
Elizabeth Hairston-Mc Burrows Ph.D, Rose of Sharon of Dance, Founder: The Apostolic Prophetic Connection, Founder, President

"I entrusted one of my songs to Tramona to interpret in dance. What a thrill it was to see it come alive! Tramona's heart for worship through dance was moving and anointed. She used her entire body to express the heart of God through my song. She interpreted my heart as a composer....and blended the music, the lyrics and her body in such a way that the Father reached into someone else's life and touched a broken place that only He knew about. Such is the power of worship through dance. She wanted no glory for herself. Rather, she yielded her gift of dance as a sweet sacrifice of worship. I applaud Tramona's vision and passion to memorialize her journey in writing to encourage others likewise called to minister through dance."
Prophet Candace L. Long-Founder, Creativity Training Institute, Inc.

My sister in Christ, Tramona Ford's testimony of her desire to know more about God and dance ministry was a great pleasure and enlightening. I've witnessed God move mightily in her life as she engaged in a thorough examination of self, her heart, attitude, and motivation. Her worship is a sacrificial offering, an effective ministry and a levitical example rooted in a strong ministry foundation.This book is full of integrity because it reflects the essence of what she exhibits publicly and who she is privately. I highly recommend this book to motivate you to examine your call, unique gifts and fragrance unto God.
Rev. Eyesha Kuturah Marable Founding Director- National Liturgical Dance Network

DEDICATION

To the Lord: Thank You for entrusting me with the gift of dance and also with the revelatory meaning and understanding so the lost will be restored, the broken will be healed, and Your love will be displayed. My prayer is that You accept my service of worship and that others may be drawn closer to You by my example.

To Greg, Steven, Shennelle, Trevor, and Jada: You have taken this journey with me. I love you more than life. I thank you for walking the road with me, whether it was late nights, extras rehearsals, or traveling near or far; you supported me through it all. I am truly blessed.

In memory of the late Pastor Troy Hopkins: Thank you for seeing the gift of dance in me and encouraging me to move in my gift.

To Pastors Wendell and Juanita Burden, who not only embraced me but started me on my journey beyond the four walls of the church building, I say thank you and I appreciate you.

To my Ecclesia sisters: Bonnie (mom), Elder Amy, Minister Pamela, Minister Mary, Annette, Carol, Jada, and Shennelle. Thank you for speaking into my life. I am eternally grateful to you for allowing me to share my most inner being with you during my journey.

To Reverend Eyesha Marble: Thank you for getting me started on this road of dance ministry. I can't thank you enough for being a great example of a leader.

To Pastor Lynn Hayden, my dance mom: Thank you for your encouraging words, your life example, your time, and your wisdom you shared with me along this journey.

To Apostle Elizabeth Hairston-McBurrows: Thank you for teaching and equipping me for true prophetic ministry.

TABLE OF CONTENTS

Fragrance:

But thanks be to God, who always leads us as captives in Christ's triumphal procession and uses us to spread the aroma of the knowledge of Him everywhere. For we are to God the pleasing aroma of Christ among those who are being saved and those who are perishing.

2 Corinthians 2:14-15

OUR WORSHIP, A SACRIFICIAL OFFERING

Therefore, I urge you, brothers and sisters, in view of God's mercy, to offer your bodies as a living sacrifice, holy and pleasing to God—this is your true and proper worship.

Romans 12:1-2

I began dancing in the church without much knowledge; all I knew is that I loved to dance. My mom would often talk about how I would just dance around the house as a little girl. I loved music and rhythm, whether it was instrumental or not.

One day I told the Lord, "I want to know more. I need to know more about dance in the church. How did it get started? Is there a place for it? I know I experience things I can't explain while dancing, but how does it all work?"

As I began to search out the answers to my many questions, I continued to dance in my private time with the Lord. See, I had been expressing myself in movement with the Lord a long time before I publicly worshipped the Lord in movement. I would just close my eyes and move. A feeling of freedom and peace would cover me like a blanket. At these times, I felt the closest to God. It truly is hard to explain verbally, but I knew in my heart it was okay and Papa loved it.

One day my private dance went public. During a Sunday morning worship service I knelt on the floor and began to worship my God. My hands began swaying back and forth, and then my hands began to interpret the words. What in the world is going on? I had been exposed, yes exposed. Once I came to myself, I couldn't believe what I had just done. Dancing publicly allows others to see you exposed before the Lord, and this can be very challenging as a dancer.

After a few weeks went by my pastor, Troy Hopkins, acknowledged my dancing and asked if I would start a dance ministry at the church. I was taken back, as this frightened me because this would force me to be intimate with the Lord openly, and I considered this my private worship time. Needless to say, after much consideration I agreed to take on the challenge.

When we dance before the Lord, we offer up our sacrifice of praise to Him. We must approach this; the same way we would as if we were the priest in biblical times, when each sacrificial offering presented to God was without spot, blemish, or defect.

The story of Cain and Abel is a prime example of not offering our best to the Lord:

> And in the course of time Cain brought to the Lord an offering of the fruit of the ground. And Abel brought of the firstborn of his flock and of the fat portions. And the Lord had respect

and regard for Abel and for his offering. But for Cain and his offering he had no respect or regard. So Cain was exceedingly angry and indignant, and he looked sad and depressed (Genesis 4:3-5).

Here we see how God was displeased with Cain's offering because it was not his first fruit. It is not mentioned here if the fruit was blemished or had a defect, but it is clearly stated that Abel brought an offering from his firstborn flock.

What am I saying? As such, we need to do a thorough examination of ourselves daily of our heart, attitude, and motivation. Our heart requires forgiveness and purity so that we can be used as a viable vehicle for the Holy Spirit to deliver the word of God through our movement.

Dance was an essential part of the Jewish life in biblical times. Dances were performed on both secular and sacred occasions. Some of these occasions were weddings, entertainment before the elite, celebrations of military victories, the return of the prodigal son; the list goes on. *"A time to weep, and a time to laugh: and a time to mourn, and a time to dance" (Ecclesiastes 3:4).*

Dancers are worshippers who express themselves through movement. Some express themselves through singing, preaching, teaching, clapping, etc. Worship is showing the creator our adoration and reverence.

It is a spiritual act, an attitude of the heart. *"I will praise the Lord with all my heart" (Psalms 9:1).* Dance is a form of worship that can and will lead you into the Holy of Holies.

Movement ministry enhances the worship experience. It gives one visual interpretation along with vocal and/or instrumental experience. *"Let them praise His name in the dance: let them sing unto Him with the timbrel and harp" (Psalms 149:3).* Each movement is one's own expression or interpretation of a word.

Each movement speaks volumes, whether good or evil, direct or indirect, hope or hopelessness, etc. So we must ask ourselves, "What does the Holy Spirit want to say to the body of Christ through my movement?" It is the Holy Spirit's voice that should be heard through our movement, not our own.

You are probably saying, "I can't always have my attitude in check!" On the contrary, I believe we can. When I feel overwhelmed, like everything is crashing down, I have to talk to myself by encouraging myself. Even in your worst moments you can find a song or a word that will lift you up. It is my desire to never allow situations to affect the condition of my heart. *"People may be pure in their own eyes, but the LORD examines their motives" (Proverbs 16:2; NLT).*

We are constantly challenged by the word of God, which sometimes seems so unobtainable. This is a lifelong journey; however, we must remain committed to the Father.

David challenges us to search ourselves deep within:

> *"Lord, who shall dwell [temporarily] in Your tabernacle? Who shall dwell [permanently] on Your holy hill? He who walks and lives uprightly and blamelessly, who works rightness and justice and speaks and thinks the truth in his heart, he who does not slander with his tongue, nor does evil to his friend, nor takes up a reproach against his neighbor; in whose eyes a vile person is despised, but he who honors those who fear the Lord (who revere and worship Him); who swears to his own hurt and does not change; [he who] does not put out his money for interest [to one of his own people] and who will not take a bribe against the innocent. He who does these things shall never be moved." (Psalm 15:1-5; AMP)*

We are the "who" and we decide if we will dwell temporarily or permanently on His holy hill. Will we live uprightly and blameless? Will we work rightness and justice? Will we speak and think the truth in our heart? Will we choose not to slander with our tongue or do evil to our friend?

I believe we often forget that Christ came to earth in human form and in His humanity He still made a choice to live by what His father spoke to Him.

11

In the midst of Christ's heartfelt distress in the garden of Gethsemane, he wanted to follow after the flesh, but He knew His purpose; therefore, He made a decision to remain committed to His call.

See, it was God's original intent and plan to be in relationship with us, not to be separated. Unfortunately, we were separated by our forefathers due to sin in the Garden of Eden.

In the garden, the presence of the Almighty never ceased. However, the day Adam chose to eat the fruit from the tree of good and evil was the day separation came on the scene (Genesis 3).

Now we have to create an atmosphere in which the Holy Spirit can come and dwell among us so that we can feel what Adam and Eve felt every day in the Garden.

Offering God our best should be our deepest desire, and we shouldn't want anything more than to please Him.

THE LEVITES: OUR EXAMPLE

In the past five years you may have heard people talk about Levites rising up in this hour. Let's talk about it.

As we study our biblical history of the Levites we find they were set apart for specific tasks within the tabernacle. The Levitical priesthood began with the tribe of Levi and proceeded through the sons of Aaron, according to Numbers 18:1-8 and Exodus 28:1. There was an exception: any male descendants of Aaron with physical blemishes were disqualified (Leviticus 21:17-23).

Why do we continue to see this statement throughout the scriptures, "no blemishes?" Does this still pertain to us today because we don't live under the law? Yes, it does apply to us today. The difference between the Old Testament and the New Testament is that Christ's blood overshadows our sin. The scriptures clearly teach the believer not to practice sin. But if we do, He is faithful and just to forgive our sins, according to 1 John 1:9.

> *"The one who practices sin is of the devil; for the devil has sinned from the beginning. The Son of God appeared for this purpose, to destroy the works of the devil. No one who is born of God practices sin, because His seed abides in him; and he cannot sin, because he is born of God. By this the children of God and the children of the devil are obvious: anyone who does not practice righteousness is not of God, nor the one who does not love his brother" (1 John 3:8-10).*

The scripture verses here make a clear distinction between those that practice sin and those that don't. Let's weigh in on the side that does not. Amen.

God chose the Old Testament Levites to live closest to His presence. But before He could dwell in their midst, they had to endure a time of refining not required of the other tribes. They were given a GREAT responsibility to take care of the tabernacle, the holy place.

1. **Gershonites**: They were the gatekeepers, carrying within them the coverings and figurative tapestries, and were charged with guarding the veils and portals used in God's presence. They were uniquely gifted in making visible and functional the place where God can manifest His glory.

2. **Kohathites:** This group was in charge of carrying, bearing, or shouldering the holy items (the ark, table of showbread, candlestick, altar of burnt offering, alter of incense, sacred vessels, and the veil separating the Holy of Holies). They were called to live closest to the presence of the Lord.

3. **Merarites:** They were responsible for all the foundational elements and setting God's presence firmly in the earth. Their gift was building and establishing the foundations to usher in the presence of God.

During the wilderness period, the Levites learned their proper roles and assignments, including how to approach God and effectively minister to His people. Just as God called the Levites then, He is calling now a new Levitical people to prepare for His return.

The Levites understood their call and unique gifts. Each group was given an assignment, and they had to perform each task precisely or they would die. Look again at each group. Do the duties of each group closely mirror the five-fold ministry, the worship team, and the dance ministry? Today we depend so much on the grace of God that we don't give our assignments much thought or protect the holy place like we should. I am sure this hurts the Father's heart more than we can imagine. Imagine your child not following your directions for a specific task. Some of us get fighting mad and punish our children for not obeying.

Not God, He will be okay. He will give me another chance. This is how we often think, sad but true. Let's work on this, and let's do better.

We must be mindful not to offend our Jewish brothers and sisters, as we know we are not Levities by our bloodline. However, God is raising a generation up that will take on their Kingdom responsibility, to embrace their calling and surrender their gifts to serve the Kingdom of Heaven.

There were five offerings discussed in Leviticus chapters 1-7. These offerings were mandated by law in the Old Testament; however, there are principles we can we learn and glean from today.

Five Levitical Offerings

1. **Burnt offering:** The burnt offering was a sacrifice that was completely burnt. None of it was to be eaten at all, and therefore the fire consumed the whole sacrifice. It is also important to note that the fire on the altar was never to go out, and it represented lifelong atonement and dedication.

2. **Grain/Meal offering:** The offering was brought to one of the priests, who took it to the altar and cast a "memorial portion" on the fire, and he did this also with the incense. The priest ate the remainder, unless he was bringing the grain offering for himself, where he would burn the whole thing. The purpose of the grain offering was an offering of gifts and speaks of a life that is dedicated to generosity and giving. Every day is a gift from God.

3. **Fellowship/Peace offering:** The offering was a meal shared with the Lord, the priests, and sometimes the common Israelites. The worshipper was to bring male or female oxen, sheep, or goats. The ritual was closely compared to the burnt offering up to the point of the actual burning, where the animal's blood was poured around the edges of the altar. The fat and entrails were burned, and the remainder was eaten by the priests and (if it was a free-will offering) by the worshippers themselves. This sacrifice of praise and thanksgiving was most of the time a voluntary act representing fellowship with God.

4. **Sin offering:** The sin offering expiated (paid the debt in full) the worshippers' unintentional weaknesses and failures before the Lord. Each class of people had various ordinances to perform. Unintentional sins were difficult to identify and could happen at any time, and therefore the priests worked closely as mediators to instruct the people as they sought the Lord. In case any sins were not brought before the Lord, there were offerings for the nation and for the high priest, which covered them all in a collective way. On the Day of Atonement (Yom Kippur) the high priest sprinkled blood on the mercy seat for his own sins and the sins of the nation.

5. **Trespass offering:** This offering was very similar to that of the sin offering, but the main difference was that it was an offering of money for sins of ignorance connected with fraud. For example, if someone unintentionally cheated another out of money or property, his sacrifice was to be equal to the amount taken, plus one-fifth to the priest and to the one offended. Therefore he repaid twice the amount taken, plus 40%.

Every offering is a clear picture of Christ. Each of the five Levitical offerings was a finger pointing to Christ, and He was each of them.

Based on biblical history we see how important it was and still is to be holy and pure before a Holy God. Despite the fall in Genesis, it is through Christ we have been reconciled back to the Father. And because of this we no longer need a priest to take a sacrifice to God for us, but instead are able to come boldly before Him for ourselves. Hallelujah!

Through the vehicle of dance we are charged by Holy Scripture to walk upright if we want to abide in the tabernacle and be used by the Holy Spirit the way God desires.

IMPORTANCE OF A STRONG MINISTRY FOUNDATION

And the LORD answered me, and said, Write the vision, and make it plain upon tables, that he may run that readeth it. For the vision is yet for an appointed time, but at the end it shall speak, and not lie: though it tarry, wait for it; because it will surely come, it will not tarry.

Habakkuk 2:2-3

It is important that your ministry team has a solid foundation on which the members can build. You will find when expectations are written and understood that it takes the guessing and stress out of the equation for the ministry leader and members of the team.

After writing your vision and plan, this should be reviewed with the pastor(s) of the house and receive approval before moving forward. Without the pastor's approval ministry will not take place. Many pastors and lay members struggle regarding the ministry of arts in the church. Unfortunately, many are not educated regarding the word concerning movement ministry or they just don't believe dance ministry is for today in the local church.

The Bible clearly identifies what our position should be, whether 2000 years ago or today.

> *"In the beginning God created the heavens and the earth. Now the earth was formless and empty, darkness covered the surface of the watery depths, and the Spirit of God was hovering over the surface of the waters." (Genesis 1:1-2)*

The Holy Spirit hovered and moved over the surface of the earth. Time began with movement. We express ourselves in movement daily. It is the first sign of life and vitality even in our mother's womb. When embryos are moving, doctors and parents are confident they are doing well. When there is little or no movement, concern is raised. From the beginning of our existence we are predestined to move our limbs and to respond to sound. Yet in the most holy place, when it's time for us to experience God, the creator of all things, of all men, we lose our agility and become lifeless.

The same holds true outside the womb. Movement is pivotal to the vitality of a person. If expressiveness was commissioned by God as an integral part of our life experience, then why would He exclude it when communing with Him? He wouldn't. Dance and movement are necessary in the life of a church, especially when trying to appeal to and nurture a young population. This can be done without compromise.

Things to consider when writing a ministry standard:

1. Vision and mission.

2. Rehearsal expectations.

3. Garment, make-up, and worship instruments (who is responsible for purchase).

4. Monthly offering.

5. Outside engagements.

6. Forms: parental consent, application (area of ministry interest). Parent and participants should sign forms for accountability.

7. Pastor's expectations: corporate worship, how many times per month would they like to have a special dance; traveling with pastors when they are invited to preach for outside engagements.

8. What are the requirements to join the team?

9. Can anyone join the team?

Your rehearsals should consist of a balance between bible study, warm-up exercises, movement exercises, concepts, a specific choreographed piece, and getting comfortable with worship instruments. Remember, it takes time to develop a strategy, but you must start somewhere. And as the ministry grows, adjustments will need to be made.

There is a portion in my ministry standard that clearly states, "if you miss the last two rehearsals before a presentation you will not be able to participate in the presentation." I was faced with reminding a parent that she signed the accountability agreement, and her son was unable to participate in the Easter presentation because of missed practices. This was hard to face especially when dealing with children, but we must hold members and parents accountable to establish order and integrity for the ministry.

I believe we as dance leaders are responsible for those who follow us. Our role is just as important as a pastor. We are the example they will follow.

We have been set apart to teach how to lead others in worship. We are much like the Levites who were responsible for the altar and brought the sacrifices to be burnt offerings unto the Lord. We must not take lightly the charge we have been given. Remember you, the leader, are building the offering that will go up before the Lord. Will God be pleased with your fragrance?

Once a solid foundation is built, continue building.

EFFECTIVE MINISTRY

You will be effective if you affect your ministry.

The fruit will grow if you cultivate the ground, feed and water it properly.

How can we ensure our ministry is effective? I am glad you asked. Over the years I have found that we don't truly know how effective we are until we receive feedback from others or see results. However, you can ensure ministry effectiveness if you diligently seek the Lord in prayer, study the bible for biblical examples and instructions, seek out a mentor that will share his or her wisdom, and keep ministry issues real.

Ministry, as you may know, is not an easy task. Many challenges come with any call to leadership. We must bear a lot and carry the yoke of others as well as our own. We have to learn much self-discipline, which is not easy.

Our character and integrity are very important. Our character defines who we are.

> *"Therefore, since we have been justified by faith, we have peace with God through our Lord Jesus Christ. Through Him we have also obtained access by faith into this grace in which we stand, and we rejoice in*

hope of the glory of God. Not only that, but we rejoice in our sufferings, knowing that suffering produces endurance, and endurance produces character, and character produces hope, and hope does not put us to shame, because God's love has been poured into our hearts through the Holy Spirit who has been given to us" (Romans 5:1-5; ESV).

No matter how you slice the fruit, it's still a fruit. People know us by our character. Ministry comes at a cost, but if we persevere it proves us. The Lord wants us to be consistent in our actions and reactions according to His word. If we continue to pursue Him, He will show up through you and me as His hands to touch those who are in need of Him.

For example,

Prophetic dance:

I've had several experiences over the years in which I have danced prophetically. Most recently, during a Sunday morning service my pastor asked me to dance around one of the female members of our church. As I began dancing around her, her husband came and stood behind her. As the Holy Spirit led, I grabbed her husband's hands above her head and we began a motion up and down the sides of her body and over her head. We continued this motion until I felt released. As her husband followed me in movement the Holy Spirit said, "cover her, you must cover her more than you have." He followed me so fluidly. What an experience. This was the first time I had the opportunity to minister to a couple.

About three years ago I was asked by my pastor to dance after she preached at a women's conference. During the dance I moved out into the crowd and began ministering through dance to individuals. After service, there was an elderly woman who approached me and said she was not going to come to service because she just didn't feel well but she had changed her mind. She expressed how glad she was that she did not miss the ministry because she no longer felt sick after I ministered to her in dance. How powerful is that?!

Prophetic dance is simply expressing the Father's heart to a person or persons.

Prophetic dance can be very challenging for someone who has never experienced one-on-one interaction with someone while dancing. When dancing corporately, you don't have to look anyone in the face or come close to the people. However, during prophetic ministry you must be led, you must look people in their eyes, and you must connect with them in that moment as the Father seeks to meet them right where they are. Dancing in the prophetic is not necessarily as deep as some may think or believe, but I do believe it's important to allow the Holy Spirit to lead you to those He wants to speak to at that moment in time.

I believe just as there are prophesies for the corporate body, there are also prophesies for individuals, and when we minister in prophetic dance we must approach it the same way.

"For in Him we live and move and have our being" (Acts 17:28; NIV).

Corporate worship/Unity in motion:

Unity in the body of Christ is vital, and when we are in one accord the gifts of the spirit will flow during our services. We as dancers accompany our praise and worship teams to shift the atmosphere of the service for the gifts to manifest so the needs of the people are met.

Congregational movement should be easy to follow, not just for the dancers but also for the congregation. The lead dancer should use a combination of 3 to 4 fluid movements during the entire song. This fluidity will allow for easy following and for the Holy Spirit to move during praise and worship.

> *"Complete my joy by being of the same mind, having the same love, being in full accord and of one mind"* (Philippians 2:2).

"I appeal to you, brothers, by the name of our Lord, Jesus Christ, that all of you agree, and that there be no divisions among you, but that you be united in the same mind and the same judgment" (1 Corinthians 1:10).

What we offer unto the Lord will be released in our services. The fire we offer will come from the lifestyle we live. If we live a lifestyle of worship our offering will not be "strange fire".

> *"Aaron's sons Nadab and Abihu put coals of fire in their incense burners and sprinkled incense over them. In this way, they disobeyed the LORD by burning before him the wrong kind of fire, different than he had commanded" Leviticus 10:1.*

One day, two of Aaron's sons, Nadab and Abihu, came along and offered incense with "strange fire." The Hebrew word translated "strange" means "unauthorized, foreign, or profane." God not only rejected their sacrifice; He found it so offensive that He consumed the two men with fire.

In judging Nadab and Abihu for their strange fire, God was making a point to all the other priests who would serve in His tabernacle—and later, in His temple—and to us, as well. Since this was the first time sacrifices were being offered on the altar and Israel was getting to know the living God better, when Aaron's sons were disobedient and profane, God displayed His displeasure in no uncertain terms. God was not going to allow the disobedience of Aaron's sons to set a precedent for future disregard of His Law.

Whatever it was the men did to render the offering profane; it was a sign of their disregard for the utter holiness of God and the need to honor and obey Him in solemn and holy fear. Their carelessness and irreverence were their downfall.

Again, what we offer unto the Lord will be released in our services. The fire we offer will come from the lifestyle we live. If we live a lifestyle of worship our offering will not be "strange fire".

You will know how effective or ineffective you are during corporate worship by feeling the shift in the atmosphere yourself, by watching the change in the service, by watching others join in movement, or by someone simply telling you how blessed they were by your ministry.

Conclusion

"Therefore be imitators of God, as beloved children; 2 and walk in love, just as Christ also loved you and gave Himself up for us, an offering and a sacrifice to God as a fragrant aroma. 3 But immorality or any impurity or greed must not even be named among you, as is proper among saints" Ephesians 5:1

We must not be conformed to the world's mindset as this will change over time. But we must remember that we serve a Holy God who is the same yesterday, today, and forevermore that wants a Holy sacrifice. We are the Holy sacrifice!

There will be remnant of people in the last days that will stand firm on the word of God. This remnant will keep the altar Holy and choose to live Holy lives.

Saints, what I am saying? We are to be imitators of Christ, our perfect example. He served and offered His best while in His humanity. Christ was our perfect sacrifice. Christ's fragrant aroma should be sensed by those around us, whether at work, on the playground, on the basketball court, at the gym, or in the park.

Let the fragrance of Heaven permeate your area of influence.

The fragrance of your dance will shift the atmosphere of worship to an atmosphere of liberty, healing, and deliverance.

BIBLOGRAPHY

BIBLE VERSIONS

NEW KING JAMES VERSION

NEW LIVING TRANSLATION

ENGLISH STANDARD VERSION

THE LEVITICAL CALLING by Candace Long

National Liturgical Dance Network-Founder, Rev. Eyesha Marable

gotquestions.org

BIOGRAPHY

Tramona Ford is a licensed, ordained minister of the gospel and the ministry of arts director under Pastors Dr. Wendell and Dr. Juanita Burden at Family Life Ministries International in York, PA. She has been ministering in dance for 11+ years in her local area and has also traveled internationally to teach. Tramona is married with four children. She enjoys not just helping others but serving her community.

Tramona began her training under Reverend Eyesha Marble, founder of the National Liturgical Network and a graduate of Dancing for Him Ministries on-line school founded by Pastor Lynn Hayden. She has also trained in prophetic ministry under Apostle Elizabeth Hairston-McBurrows, founder of the Apostolic-Prophetic Connections. Tramona's desire is not only to express the heart of God to the lost but to encourage the body of Christ through the visual arts. She has a unique way of combining dance and drama to her ministry.

She has been sought out by local ministries to teach and train ministry of arts teams as they pursue their desire to minister more effectively in and with liturgical dance. Tramona's desire is to see ministries have a strong biblical foundation so they are equipped to minister effectively. Tramona also enjoys traveling for missions. She loves people and her goal has always been to teach, equip, encourage, and uplift the body of Christ.

Printed in Great Britain
by Amazon